Read-

Living Near the Wetland

By Donna Loughran

Consultant
Nanci R. Vargus, Ed.D.
Assistant Professor of Literacy
University of Indianapolis, Indianapolis, Indiana

Children's Press®
A Division of Scholastic Inc.
New York   Toronto   London   Auckland   Sydney
Mexico City   New Delhi   Hong Kong
Danbury, Connecticut

Designer: Herman Adler Design
Photo Researcher: Caroline Anderson
The photo on the covers shows Titcomb Basin.

Library of Congress Cataloging-in-Publication Data

Loughran, Donna.
 Living near the wetland / by Donna Loughran.
  p. cm. – (Rookie read-about geography)
Summary: Introduces the wetland environment and some of the people and
animals that dwell in wetlands.
 ISBN 0-516-22741-6 (lib. bdg.)   0-516-27332-9 (pbk.)
 1. Wetlands–Juvenile literature. [1. Wetlands.] I. Title. II.
Series.
 QH87.3.L68 2003
 578.768–dc21

                                   2003003897

Squish, squish.
Wiggle your toes.

Smell the water.
See the grass move.

Red-winged blackbird

Hear the birds cry.
You are in a wetland.

Cattails

Look at the cattails. Their
tops are fuzzy and brown.

Listen to the loud noise.
A bullfrog is hiding in
the cattails.

Do you live near a wetland?
Many people do.

It is a place between land
and water.

Most wetlands have water all year. The water can be fresh or salty.

Sometimes the water moves slowly. Sometimes it does not move at all.

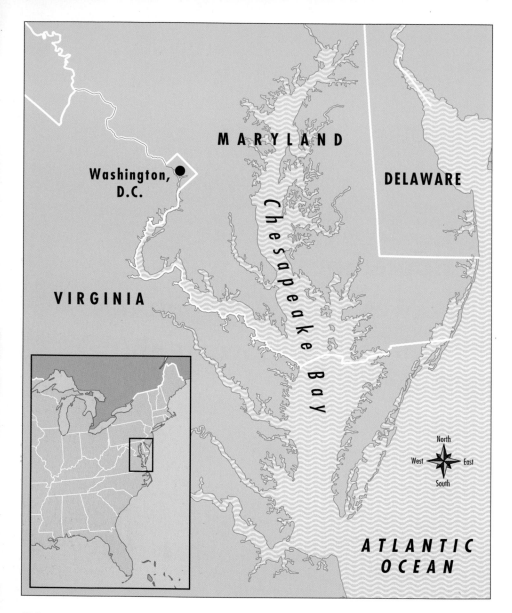

Marshes and swamps are kinds of wetlands. These wetlands are around Chesapeake (CHE-sah-peek) Bay.

Swamp

Animals live in these wetlands, too. In the winter, there are ducks and geese. There are otters, beavers, and songbirds all year long.

River otters

Beaver

People come to Chesapeake Bay to see all of the animals.

Oysters

Many fish grow up in the wetlands. Oysters (OI-sterz) do, too. Oysters live between two hard shells.

Fish and oysters are important to fishermen on Chesapeake Bay.

The Camargue (kuh-MARG) is a wetland in France.

UNITED KINGDOM

BELGIUM

GERMANY

LUXEMBOURG

FRANCE

SWITZERLAND

North
West   East
South

ATLANTIC OCEAN

Rhone River

ITALY

Camargue

SCALE 1 inch = 120 miles

0   Miles   120

0   Kilometers   190

SPAIN

Mediterranean Sea

Wild bulls and white
horses eat grasses in
the fields there.

Muskrats swim next to
paths where people walk.

Eagles and hawks fly in the sky.

Red-tailed hawk

Rice field

Farmers grow fruit and wheat. They grow rice in the wet fields.

People wait for ponds
filled with ocean water
to dry.

Then, they collect the salt.

Salt

Flamingoes

There is a bird park in Camargue.

People come to see owls, hawks, storks, and swans. They also see beautiful pink flamingoes.

Squish, squish.
Wiggle your toes.

Is there a wetland
near you?

Words You Know

bullfrog

cattails

flamingoes

marsh

otters

oyster

swamp

Index

About the Author

Donna Loughran is a freelance writer, artist, and multimedia designer. She lives in Austin, Texas.

Photo Credits

Photographs © 2003: Corbis Images: 21 (Eric and David Hosking), 3 (Paul A. Souders); Dembinsky Photo Assoc.: 16, 31 top right (E.R. Degginger), 10 (Terry Donnelly), 13, 31 bottom (Bill Lea), cover (Richard Hamilton Smith), 5 (George E. Stewart); Folio, Inc.: 15, 20 (Middleton Evans), 14, 31 top left (John A. Sawyer); ImageState/Miwako Ball: 25; Masterfile/Janet Foster: 7, 30 top left; Omni-Photo Communications/Lorri Goodman: 4; Peter Arnold Inc./Jeff Greenberg: 9; Photo Researchers, NY: 29 (Larry L. Miller), 6, 30 top right (Hans Reinhard/Okapia), 19 (Leonard Lee Rue III); Stock Boston/David Ulmer: 17; The Image Works/Sondra Dawes: 30 bottom right; TRIP Photo Library: 22 (H. Rogers), 26, 30 bottom left (B. Turner).

Maps by Bob Italiano